Five Naughty Kittens

A rhyming
counting story

First published in 2004 by
Franklin Watts
96 Leonard Street
London
EC2A 4XD

Franklin Watts Australia
45–51 Huntley Street
Alexandria
NSW 2015

Text © Martyn Beardsley 2004
Illustration © Jacqueline East 2004

A CIP catalogue record for this book is available
from the British Library.

ISBN 0 7496 5306 X (hbk)
ISBN 0 7496 5370 1 (pbk)

Series Editor: Jackie Hamley
Series Advisors: Dr Barrie Wade, Dr Hilary Minns
Design: Peter Scoulding

Printed in Hong Kong / China

Five Naughty
Kittens

Written by
Martyn Beardsley

Illustrated by
Jacqueline East

W
FRANKLIN WATTS
LONDON•SYDNEY

Martyn Beardsley
"I love writing and reading stories. I like spooky stories best. I also like football and other sports. I hope you enjoy the book!"

Jacqueline East
"I have a puppy who is just as naughty as these kittens – he loves chasing frogs and eating my garden!"

Five naughty kittens
play in the drawer.

Oh no!

Now there are four!

Four naughty kittens
climb up the tree.

Oh no!

Now there are three!

Three naughty kittens
hide in the shoe.

12

Oh no!

Now there are two!

Two naughty kittens
stretch in the sun.

Oh no!

Now there's just one!

One lonely kitten
cries for the others.

21

Hurray! Back together,
sisters and brothers.

23

Notes for parents and teachers

READING CORNER has been structured to provide maximum support for new readers. The stories may be used by adults for sharing with young children. Primarily, however, the stories are designed for newly independent readers, whether they are reading these books in bed at night, or in the reading corner at school or in the library.

Starting to read alone can be a daunting prospect. READING CORNER helps by providing visual support and repeating words and phrases, while making reading enjoyable. These books will develop confidence in the new reader, and encourage a love of reading that will last a lifetime!

If you are reading this book with a child, here are a few tips:

1. Make reading fun! Choose a time to read when you and the child are relaxed and have time to share the story.

2. Encourage children to reread the story, and to retell the story in their own words, using the illustrations to remind them what has happened.

3. Give praise! Remember that small mistakes need not always be corrected.

READING CORNER covers three grades of early reading ability, with three levels at each grade. Each level has a certain number of words per story, indicated by the number of bars on the spine of the book, to allow you to choose the right book for a young reader:

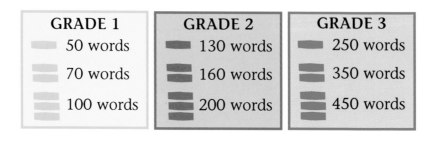

GRADE 1	GRADE 2	GRADE 3
50 words	130 words	250 words
70 words	160 words	350 words
100 words	200 words	450 words

Terry the Flying Turtle

First published 2005
Evans Brothers Limited
2A Portman Mansions
Chiltern St
London W1U 6NR

British Library Cataloguing in Publication Data

Wilson, Anna
         Terry the Flying Turtle. - (Zig zags)
         1. Children's stories - Pictorial works
         I. Title
         823.9'14 [J]

ISBN 0 237 52849 5

Printed in China by WKT Company Limited

Series Editor: Nick Turpin
Design: Robert Walster
Production: Jenny Mulvanny
Series Consultant: Gill Matthews

Terry the Flying Turtle

by Anna Wilson

illustrated by Mike Gordon

Evans

"I'm clever," said Terry the Turtle. Polly the Chimp laughed.

Terry was cross.
"I **am** clever," said Terry.
"I can fly."

6

Polly laughed and laughed.
"You can't fly!" she said.

Terry was cross.
"I **can** fly," he said.
"You'll see."

"Will you help me?"
Terry asked the parrot.
"I want to fly."

13

14

The parrot
laughed.
Terry was cross.
"Please will
you help me?"
he asked.

"Alright," said the parrot. "Hold this twig and I'll hold it too."

16

"Why?" asked Terry.

"Because it will help you fly,"
said the parrot.

The parrot held on.
Terry held on.

The parrot flew.
Terry flew!

23

The animals watched.
"Look at Terry!" they said.
"He looks silly!"

Terry was cross.
"I'm not silly," he shouted.
"You're silly. I'm flying!"

Terry fell
down and
down.

SPLASH!

"You look silly now!" Polly said.

Why not try reading another ZigZag book?

Dinosaur Planet   ISBN 0 237 52793 6
by David Orme and Fabiano Fiorin

Tall Tilly   ISBN 0 237 52794 4
by Jillian Powell and Tim Archbold

Batty Betty's Spells   ISBN 0 237 52795 2
by Hilary Robinson and Belinda Worsley

The Thirsty Moose   ISBN 0 237 52792 8
by David Orme and Mike Gordon

The Clumsy Cow   ISBN 0 237 52790 1
by Julia Moffatt and Lisa Williams

Open Wide!   ISBN 0 237 52791 X
by Julia Moffatt and Anni Axworthy

Too Small   ISBN 0 237 52777 4
by Kay Woodward and Deborah van de Leijgraaf

I Wish I Was An Alien   ISBN 0 237 52776 6
by Vivian French and Lisa Williams

The Disappearing Cheese   ISBN 0 237 52775 8
by Paul Harrison and Ruth Rivers

Terry the Flying Turtle   ISBN 0 237 52774 X
by Anna Wilson and Mike Gordon

Pet To School Day   ISBN 0 237 52773 1
by Hilary Robinson and Tim Archbold

The Cat in the Coat   ISBN 0 237 52772 3
by Vivian French and Alison Bartlett